The
Blind
Colt

Written and Illustrated
by GLEN ROUNDS

SCHOLASTIC BOOK SERVICES

NEW YORK • TORONTO • LONDON • AUCKLAND • SYDNEY

For My Father

Copyright 1941, 1960 by Holiday House, Inc. This edition is published by Scholastic Book Services, a division of Scholastic Magazines, Inc., by arrangement with Holiday House, Inc.

4th printing . . . . January 1970

Printed in the U.S.A.

Contents

The Badlands

It was near sundown of an early spring afternoon when the brown mustang mare left the wild horse band where it grazed on the new spring grass, and climbed carefully to the top of a nearby hogback.

All afternoon she had been restless and nervous, spending much of her time on high ground watching the country around her. Now she stood and stamped her feet fretfully while she tipped her sharp-pointed ears forward and back as she looked and listened. Her nostrils flared wide as she tested the wind for any smells that might be about.

The rain-gullied buttes and pinnacles of the Badlands threw long black shadows across the soft gray and brown and green of the alkali flats below her. A few jack rabbits had already left their hiding places and were prospecting timidly around in the open, searching out the tender

5

shoots of new grass. They, too, threw long black shadows that were all out of proportion to their size.

A few bull bats boomed overhead, and a meadow lark sang from the top of a sagebrush nearby. Below her the rest of the mustang band grazed quietly, except for an occasional squeal and thump of hoofs as some minor dispute was settled. Otherwise everything was quiet.

But still the little mare didn't leave the ridge. She stood watching while the flats grew darker and the darkness crept up the sides of the buttes, until at last the sun touched only the very tiptops of the highest pinnacles. Then after a look back to where the rest of the horses were bedding down for the night, she slipped quietly down the far side of the ridge and was soon hidden in the darkness.

Next morning she was in a grassy hollow at the head of a dry coulee where the rolling prairie and the Badlands meet. And lying at her feet, sound asleep, was her colt that had been born during the night.

The early sun touched the top of the rimrock behind her, then gradually crept down until it was warming the grass where the little mustang lay. As soon as the ground had begun to steam and the touch of frost was out of the air, she nudged him with her muzzle and waked him. For a little while he lay there, sniffing around in the grass as far as he could reach, and flapping his tail to hear it thump against the ground, while the mare stood relaxed on three legs and watched him.

But after a while she seemed to figure it was time for him to be up and about, so she urged him to his feet. He was as awkward-looking a scamp as you'd care to see as he stood with his long, knobby legs braced wide apart and caught his breath after the effort of getting up.

His body was close-knit and compact, and his back was flat and strong. His muzzle was delicately shaped, but his forehead bulged as all colts' do. His neck was so short he couldn't get his nose closer to the ground than his knees, and his legs were so long he seemed to be walking on stilts. His ears were trim and sharply pointed, but looked as though they should belong to a horse much larger than he.

The mare saw all this, but she knew that colts

were put together so, and that those extra-long legs of his were specially made that way so that by the time he was a day or two old he would be able to travel as fast and as far as the grown horses in case of danger. And besides, she thought that his blue-gray coat was especially handsome.

For a few minutes the colt was busy trying to balance himself on his legs while he sniffed and snorted at everything in reach. As long as he stood still he was all right, but when he tried walking he found he was engaged in a mighty ticklish business, what with his being so high in the air with nothing holding him up but those four knobby legs. They had to be lifted and swung just so, or they got all tangled up and started him kiting off in some entirely unexpected direction.

But he was hungry, and the only way he could get anything to eat was to go after it himself; so it wasn't long before he was able to scramble around against the mare's side. After a little nuzzling around he found her teats and settled down to sucking noisily, flapping his tail with excitement.

8

Before long his sides began to stick out, he was so full of milk, and he was quite ready to enjoy the business of having his coat groomed by the mustang mare. She was fair bursting with pride, as this was her first colt. She whickered softly and caressed him with her muzzle every now and again as she scrubbed him with her rough tongue. When she hit a ticklish spot he'd flap his tail and squirm and snort his tiny snorts. When he did that she'd nip him gently with her big yellow teeth to warn him that wild young ones must learn to obey, and he'd better stand still until she was done or he might get worse.

And not an inch of his hide did she overlook. The white snip on his nose, his speckled blue sides and flanks, his legs that shaded down to black shiny hoofs: all got their share of combing and washing. By the time he had been thoroughly polished the sun was warm in the hollow and he practiced his walking again, and his smelling, and his hearing.

He started taking little exploring trips, a few wobbly steps in one direction, then another, with much snuffing and snorting as the brittle last

year's grass crackled under foot. As he got the hang of operating his walking apparatus more smoothly, he became bolder and extended the range of his explorations until sometimes he traveled as far as ten or twenty feet from the brown mare's side.

His black-tipped, pointed ears were fixed to turn in all directions, to help him locate the source of sounds he heard. He pointed them forward and back, and the soft wind that springs up on the desert in the morning brushed against them, feeling sweet and clear and smooth. What few sounds he heard at first seemed to float separately through the warm silence, as though there was all the time in the world and no need for two noises to be moving at the same time. Meadow larks whistled from nearby sagebrush, and far off he heard the harsh bickering of magpies as they quarreled over a dead rabbit or a gopher.

Later on he discovered that down close to the ground there was a thin blanket of bug sounds. Flies buzzed and grasshoppers whirled. And buryer beetles made clicking noises as they busily buried a small dead snake.

Sniffing through his nose, he caught the sharp clean smell of the sagebrush, and the more pungent smell of the greasewood as the sun began to heat it up. Occasionally he got a whiff of wild plum and chokecherry blossoms from the thicket down below the rim of the Badlands.

Of course these were the big plain smells, easily discovered. Later on he would learn to identify others that had to be searched for with flared nostrils, and carefully and delicately sifted for the story they could tell him of friends, or danger, or the location of water holes in the dry times. But for now the simpler lessons were enough to keep him busy, and the mustang mare was mighty proud of him.

But for all her pride, she was a little troubled, too. For there was something strange about the colt, although she couldn't tell exactly what the matter was. He was as lively as you'd expect any colt only a few hours old to be. He snorted and kicked up his heels when a ground squirrel whistled close by. And when a tumbleweed blew against his legs he put on a mock battle, rearing up and lashing out with his front feet. When he came back to her from his trips he'd pinch her

11

with his teeth, and pretend to fight, as any healthy colt should. But nonetheless, she felt that something was wrong.

The sun climbed higher, and the colt finally tired himself out and lay down to doze at the mare's feet. She thought about starting back to join the mustang band, but it seemed so safe and peaceful here in the pocket that she hated to leave. By tomorrow the colt's legs would be stronger and he would be able to follow her with no difficulty.

But before the morning was half gone she heard the sound of danger, an iron-shod hoof striking a stone, and looked up to see two cowboys between her and the mouth of the pocket.

It was Uncle Torwal and Whitey out to see how their range stock was getting along. Torwal was a slow-speaking fellow with a droopy red moustache, and a good many of the horses running in the Badlands belonged to him. Whitey, who was probably ten years old or thereabouts, had lived with him on the ranch for several years. Almost since he could remember. He wore a castoff Stetson hat of Torwal's and high-heeled rid-

ing boots from the same source. They lived alone like any two old sourdoughs and were a familiar sight at all the roundups, and in town of a Saturday, Torwal on a crop-eared black and Whitey on a pot-bellied old pinto named Spot. Torwal usually spoke of Whitey as his "sawed-off" foreman.

The little mare had whirled to face them, keeping the colt behind her. With her teeth bared and her ears laid back, she looked half wolf for sure.

"Spunky crittur, ain't she?" Whitey remarked as they rode carefully around, trying to get a good look at the colt.

"She's a wolf all right," Torwal agreed. "An' if you ain't careful she's agoin' to paste you plumb outta your saddle. Better not crowd her."

They sat on their horses and watched a while and admired the colt. "Purty as a picture, ain't he, Uncle Torwal?" said Whitey. "Reckon we better take him home so the wolves won't get him?"

"Don't reckon we'll take him anywheres," Torwal told him. "Looks like I'm a-goin' to have to shoot him."

13

"Shoot him! Why?" squalled Whitey. "Why he's the purtiest colt on the ranch!"

"Better look him over closer, Bub," said Torwal. "See if you notice anything outta the way about him."

"I don't see anything wrong, myself," Whitey told him, after he'd walked Spot in a circle around the mare and colt again. "He looks to me just like the kind of crittur I'd like to have for a 'Sunday' horse."

"Look at his eyes; they're white," Torwal growled. "That colt's blind as a bat!"

"Aw, them's just china eyes, Uncle Torwal," Whitey said. "Lotsa horses has china eyes. Even ol' Spot has one."

"Them ain't no china eyes, not by a long shot," said Torwal. "If you look close you'll see that they're pure white without no center. He's blind, and we gotta shoot him. Otherwise he'll fall in a hole somewheres or get wolf et."

"Well, even if he is blind do we *hafta* shoot him?" Whitey asked. "Couldn't I take him home an' keep him at the ranch?"

"All he'd be is a mess of trouble even if you got

14

him home, and I doubt that he'd go that far without somethin' happening to him anyways," Torwal told him. "An' besides, he wouldn't be good
for nothing."

"Well anyway, do we hafta shoot him?"
Whitey said. "Couldn't we just let him go loose?"

"Now quit your squallin'," Torwal told him,
patiently. "I don't like it any more than you do,
but if we leave him he'll either fall in a hole and
starve or else he'll get wolf et. Lookit her tracks
where she circled during the night. Fighting off
an ol' 'gray,' I bet she was."

While Whitey sat with his lip hanging down
almost to his collar, Torwal took another chew
from his plug and got his rifle out of his saddle
scabbard. But whenever he tried to get near the
colt the little mare was there, lashing out with her
hoofs and showing her teeth to bite either man or
horse that got too near. Before long she was covered with lather and her eyes showed white, and
the ground was plowed and trampled in a circle.
But still the colt was safe.

Then Whitey spoke up again. "Lissen, Uncle
Torwal," he said. "Lookit the way she fights. I

15

don't believe any wolf could get to that colt, the way she uses them heels. If you'll let him go I'll watch mighty close to see if he falls in anything. I'll ride out every day to see that he's all right. An' if he does fall in I — I — I'll shoot him myself!"

Uncle Torwal thought the matter over awhile.

"You want that colt mighty bad, don't yuh?" he said at last.

"Yeah, I sure do! He's the purtiest thing I've ever seen!" said Whitey. "I don't think anything will happen to him, really, Uncle Torwal! He's too smart-lookin'!"

"Well, I tell yuh," Torwal said, doubtfully. "Since you feel like that about it we'll let him go awhile. We'll be a-ridin' over here every day for a while, anyways, so we can always shoot him later.

"But don't go gettin' your hopes up," he added. "The chances are he won't last a week. An' if he does he ain't good for nothing except to eat up good grass an' be a gunny sack full of trouble."

"Nothing is going to happen to him," Whitey exclaimed. "You'll see."

16

"Maybe," said Uncle Torwal, but Whitey could see that he was glad to have an excuse for not shooting the colt. Uncle Torwal put his rifle back in the scabbard, and they sat for a minute watching the colt, and then rode off to attend to their other affairs.

The little mare watched them until they were out of sight, and finally when she could no longer hear them she turned to the colt. She nuzzled him all over to make sure that nothing had happened to him. Then, after letting him suck again, she started down the trail toward the place she'd left the mustang band, with the blind colt following close against her flank.

Sounds and Smells

Back with the mustang band, the brown mare and the blind colt settled into the routine of range life. Early mornings they moved to their favorite feeding grounds where they grazed until the sun got hot, when they dozed and rested. Late afternoons they grazed slowly towards some nearby water hole for their daily drink.

The blind colt began learning the thousands and one things that a colt must know before he can take care of himself. Because he was blind he not only had to learn the things all colts must learn, but many others besides. For a week or so he stuck pretty close to the mare's side, and she saw to it that they stayed out where the ground was level with nothing for the colt to run into.

So it was only natural that he soon came to the conclusion that all the world was flat, and that he could travel safely anywhere.

18

What he did not know was that this Badlands country was criss-crossed and honeycombed with gulleys and washouts of every size, shape, and description, and that sooner or later he would have to learn about them.

And sure enough, before long he did. It came about one morning when the horses were grazing on a grassy bench between gray shale bluffs on one side and a deep gulley on the other. The blind colt had wandered off a little farther than usual, when the mare looked up and whinnied sharply for him to come back. He had learned that she usually punished him with her big teeth when he disobeyed, but he was feeling spooky this morning, and figured that a little gallop the way he was going before he turned and came back wouldn't really be disobeying. So he flirted his tail over his back, snorted as loud as he could, and made a few buck jumps straight ahead. The third jump sent him over the edge of the gulley, and he found there was no more solid ground under his feet! •

The sensation was one he never did forget. He turned head over heels and rolled to the bottom,

19

unhurt but considerably shaken up, and thoroughly frightened. After he had picked himself up he whinnied shrilly and stood trembling and snorting until the mare came to the edge of the bank. She made comforting noises to him. With her encouragement he soon found a place in the bank where he could scramble back up to where she stood.

For several days after that he stayed almost as close as if he had been glued to the brown mare's side, and carefully felt out the ground ahead at every step. He was afraid it would fall away from under him again.

But after a few days his curiosity got the better of his fear, and he cautiously started exploring again. He soon discovered that it wasn't enough to be careful not to fall over these banks. Sometimes they stuck up, and when he ran into them they were apt to jar the daylights out of him.

However, he learned fast. In a surprisingly short time he developed a sense that warned him of these things in his path even though he could not see them.

Whitey and Uncle Torwal, riding across the range, often saw him as he picked his way cautiously over strange ground or traveled with the rest of the horses to water, pressed up close to the brown mare's side.

"Well, he ain't got himself wolf et so far," Uncle Torwal would say.

"Nossir!" Whitey would answer. "An' he ain't a-goin' to, either. He's too smart."

Uncle Torwal would spit and say nothing.

During the late spring and early summer, the band of mustangs didn't travel much. There was plenty of grass on the flats and the water holes were nearly all full. In the cool hours of the mornings the older horses grazed quietly while the colts ran and kicked among themselves. The long middle hours of the day they spent contentedly dozing in the sun.

One or another of the mares usually was to be found a little distance from the rest, where she could keep a watchful eye on the surrounding country. When it was the brown mare who was standing guard, the colt stayed close to her side. When she looked he listened, and when she

21

listened, he listened too, and stretched his nostrils wide to smell. This way he learned many things. Things surrounding him were only Sounds and Smells, as far as he could tell. Unable to see them, they of course had no shapes. Bull bats catching bugs overhead in the evening were only Booming Sounds. Coyotes skulking around about their business of catching small rodents and robbing birds' nests were Rank Furry Smells. Jack rabbits were Furry Smells too, but smaller and dustier. The rabbits were also Small Sneezes and Thumping Noises. He learned to recognize the step of every horse in the band, and could spot the step of a strange horse immediately. He learned to tell the difference between the irregular movements of a loose horse, and the steady, purposeful gait of one ridden by a man.

The blind colt often heard Whitey and Spot go by these days, recognizing them by the lazy clop of Spot's big feet and his habit of blowing imaginary bugs out of his nose every few steps.

By the time summer came on and the band started climbing to the tops of high buttes in the middle of the day to escape the flies, the colt's

22

nose and his ears were giving him almost as good a picture of the things around him as if he'd had eyes.

Now most of these things were friendly and harmless, but the slightest taint of wolf smell, even before he knew what it was, would send him racing to his mother, stamping and snorting with excitement. For the fear of wolves has been born in the bones of horses for centuries. Before long he was to learn of other unfriendly and dangerous things.

On a drowsy afternoon in the middle of the summer, the blind colt was browsing among the broken banks of a black shale butte some distance from the other horses. In little pockets here and there were scattered bunches of grass high enough for him to reach.

He didn't really need the grass, but finding it was a sort of game. He had to work his way carefully along the rain-washed banks, exploring each projecting shelf with delicate sniffing, and when he discovered a green stalk he'd reach out his long upper lip and wrap it around the grass to get it in reach of his biting teeth.

When he succeeded in pulling up a mouthful, he'd stand and grind it busily with his small milk teeth, and flap his tail and nod his head with enjoyment.

After a time he noticed an odd smell. One that was new to him. It was sharp, but not very strong. He lowered his head and snorted his nostrils clear, to catch the new scent better. It didn't have the warmth and body of an animal smell, and yet there was something about it that frightened him a little, he didn't know why.

He stamped and snorted, but nothing happened, and there was nothing moving that he could hear. So after a little he went on with his search for grass. He had worked around a jutting shoulder of the butte when he noticed the smell was suddenly stronger and then he heard a buzzing — something like a grasshopper. But a grasshopper's buzzing had never given his skin the tingly feeling he had now. He was puzzled. He listened in all directions, pointing his ears this way and that, but the sound had stopped. As soon as he stepped forward, he heard the buzz again, and this time it was sharper and louder. It came

from somewhere on the ground nearby, but as soon as he stopped to locate it, the sound stopped. He stood motionless for several minutes, waiting for it to come again. When it didn't, he figured that whatever had made it must be gone, and returned to his search for grass.

But when he stepped forward again the buzz returned, and this time it had a nervous, angry sound. The smell was stronger, too. The colt was frightened, but hadn't been able to figure out where the sound came from; so he didn't know which way to run. He stamped his foot, and as he did there was a dry rustling and a sudden movement from under an overhanging ledge at his feet as something struck his foreleg a sharp blow. The colt snorted with terror, whirled and ran for his mother, bumping into things as he went.

He had been bitten by a rattlesnake that had crawled under the ledge for shade.

The mare fussed over him and worried about him, for in a short time he was a very sick colt indeed. His leg began to swell, and he grew sick and feverish all over. Before long he was thirsty. As he waded around in the nearby water hole he

found that the mud cooled and soothed him. By evening his leg had swollen so much he could only hobble around with great difficulty. The rest of the band went away after a time, but for several days the mare and the blind colt stayed by the edge of the water hole. The colt spent the greater part of his time standing deep in the churned-up mud while the mare grazed nearby, coming back to nuzzle him and to groom his hide with her tongue every few minutes.

In a few days the swelling began to go down. Before long he was able to travel slowly by favoring the sore leg, and they set out to find the rest of the horses. A couple of weeks more and he was about as well as ever. But after that the slightest smell of rattlesnakes was enough to set him to snorting and plunging with fear.

The Water Hole

As the summer advanced, the hot dry winds blew from the south with the heat from a thousand miles of desert, and the country turned dry and brown. The small springs with their trickles of clear water were the first to dry up. Then the smaller water holes began to show wider and wider bands of dried and trampled mud around their edges, and finally they too were completely dry.

By late August the only water to be found was in a few large sinks and behind the scattered earth dams thrown up by the ranchers to hold snow water in the spring.

Old trails that had lain hard and untracked all summer were now inches deep in dust, ground up by the hoofs of the wild horse bands and the herds of cattle on their trips to water.

With so many bands coming into the few big

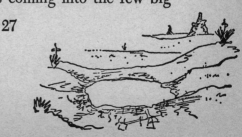

water holes, the grass near them was soon gone; so the horses had to travel farther and farther from water to feeding grounds. When the weather was cool and overcast, they sometimes went to water only once in three days. But when the hot winds blew they had to drink every day.

Before long the blind colt's band was traveling so far that the trip to water and back left little time for rest or grazing.

The blind colt was still fat and sassy, growing like a weed, but the heat and traveling were beginning to show on the brown mustang mare. Her coat had begun to look rough, and her hip bones and ribs to show.

The trips in to water were full of excitement for the colt. Early in the afternoon the band would start slowly grazing in that direction. The nearer they came to the water the shorter the grass was, having been eaten down by the stock that had passed before. After a time they'd fall into one of the well-worn paths and follow it. Before long they'd see the dust of other bunches moving in the same direction. And the last mile or so there would be flocks of sage hens plodding along in

28

single file, also on the way for their evening drink.

When they finally reached the rim overlooking the water hole, the whole band stopped while the leader looked the country over carefully. If there was another band of horses ahead of them they waited until they'd finished and gone away, for two strange bands will not drink at the same time. And, too, there was always a certain amount of danger connected with these isolated water holes. Wild horse hunters sometimes waited there, and the big gray wolves skulked about looking for a chance to pull down any animal that got trapped in the deep mud.

The blind colt enjoyed these trips, however. His ears picked up the disgruntled cluckings of the waddling sage hens, and he smelled the fresh scent of the sagebrush and any number of other pungent desert weeds drying in the hot wind. And while still a long way from the water hole, all the horses would smell the water and hurry a little faster.

When they reached the ridge, he stood with the others examining the country for danger, throwing his head high and distending his nos-

trils as far as he could. When the stallion bugled through his nose, the colt tried to do the same.

When they finally started down the trail he'd kick and squeal with excitement, nipping the flanks and hocks of whatever horse was nearest, and generally stirring up confusion.

The water hole itself always frightened him a little, for it was surrounded by a wide band of mud, dried and cracked on top, and thick and gummy under the crust. It wasn't like the nice squishy stuff he'd waded in earlier in the summer. This mud made strange sucking noises around the horses' feet and seemed to be trying to pull them down.

At first he always stayed on firm ground while the brown mare drank, waiting for her. But as the summer got drier and the colt older, the mare's supply of milk grew less and less. The colt was able to graze a little and wasn't troubled by lack of food, but he did get thirsty. One day he ventured out across the mud himself, being careful to pick a place that had been packed firmer than the rest. Except for the sucking noises around

30

his feet, nothing happened; so after that he always drank with the others.

But one day he accidentally shoved up against a short-tempered old mare and she whacked him in the ribs with her heels. The colt was startled and plunged away, landing in a boggy spot the others had been avoiding.

His hoofs, being small and sharp, didn't give him the support that the flatter ones of an older horse would have, and he felt himself sinking. The harder he tried to pull his feet loose the deeper he sank. He whinnied in terror and lunged with all his power, but all he could do was work himself deeper and deeper into the sticky mud.

The brown mare had left her drinking as soon as she heard him squall, but there was nothing she could do but nuzzle him and whicker encouragingly. By the time he was exhausted he had thrown himself partly on his side and was trapped beyond any chance of escape without help. He lay there, covered with mud, his sides heaving and his nostrils showing their red inner side.

31

The horses milled round, excited by his struggles and his frightened whinnying. After a time they all went away except the brown mare standing guard.

She stood over him and nuzzled him with her nose and wiped mud off with her tongue, comforting him as much as possible. By spells he struggled, trying to get to his feet. But after a time he wore himself out completely and just lay and shivered.

That night was the longest he'd ever known. He heard the sound of other horses coming to drink, and the squeals and thump of hoofs on ribs as the brown mare drove them off.

Somewhere in the night there was the smell of a big gray wolf prowling near, and the snorting and stamping of the mare as she circled between the blind colt and the danger.

In the morning he heard the small sounds of sage chickens and little animals drinking, but nothing else. He and the brown mare were alone. She grazed nearby, returning to the trapped colt whenever he moved or made a sound.

It was late in the morning when the mare threw

up her head to listen for a sound the colt had heard some time before. The sound of a shod horse, and from his steady gait it was plain there was a cowboy on his back. In a little while Whitey showed up on old Spot. There was much to be done these days, what with riding out to check the water holes and the like, so Torwal quite often sent him out to ride alone. And when Whitey saw the colt bogged down he was mighty glad that Torwal was not along this particular morning, because he felt sure Torwal would have argued that the colt had best be shot.

He rode up and sat a minute in his saddle while the mare watched him. This time she didn't show fight. Perhaps somehow she knew there was no need. Whitey talked soothingly to her and to the colt while he took down his rope. Shaking out a noose as he'd seen Uncle Torwal do in such cases, he rode carefully out across the mud as close as possible to the colt. The mare followed anxiously, but still not interfering. After a few unsuccessful attempts he got the loop around the colt's neck and took a dally around the saddle horn. Then, working carefully, he edged Spot

33

towards solid ground. As the noose tightened on the colt's neck he began to struggle again. But now with the pull of the rope to help him, he was soon dragged out to firm ground.

He was a messy-looking sight, with all that mud caked on him, as he lay there getting his breath. But luckily he wasn't chilled as he would have been later in the year. The brown mare trotted around like an old hen with a bunch of ducks, snorting and whinnying to herself and smelling and nudging the colt. Working very carefully and without getting out of his saddle, Whitey shook the muddy noose from the colt's neck and rode off a few yards to watch.

For a while the colt was content to lie on the grass and rest while the mare nosed him over to see if he was all right, and licked the mud off his coat. But after being in the mud all night he was mighty hungry, so it wasn't long before he struggled to his feet. His legs were pretty wobbly under him, but beyond that he didn't seem to be damaged any. And by the time the mare had nursed him and polished him from head to foot he looked and felt about as good as new, so they

34

started slowly up the trail the way the other horses had gone.

All this time Whitey had quietly watched them from a distance, with his chest thrown out and as near strutting as is possible for a fellow sitting on a sleepy old pinto horse to be. He'd been busting for some time to get a chance to pull a bogged crittur out of the mud by himself. For it to be his blind colt was almost more excitement than he could hold!

After the mare and colt had disappeared over the ridge he managed to get his attention back on his business, and climbed down to clean the mud off his rope before he coiled it back on the saddle.

When that was finished he cocked his hand-me-down Stetson as far on one side as it would go and rode away, admiring his shadow more than a little. He kind of hoped he'd get a chance to rope a wolf or some such thing to sort of finish his day out right.

The Gray Wolves

With the beginning of fall, things were more pleasant for the horses. The hot wind stopped blowing and a few early rains soon filled some of the smaller water holes, so the bands could graze farther out on the flats where the grass was high and rich.

The days began to be filled with the rustling of tumbleweeds rolling across the land and the popping and scraping of dry seed pods on the weeds.

The colt couldn't see all this, but by now he was used to keeping track of things with his nose and his ears. The tumbleweeds to him were rattly rustlings and soft, ploppy swishes as they rolled and bounced. The prairie dogs were small oily smells and querulous barks. The little piles of grass they cut and piled up to cure before dragging them into their dens were cushiony spots under his feet. The badgers, busy digging up

36

ground squirrels and mice as they fattened themselves for the winter, were rank, bristly smells and ill-natured grunts and growls scuffling along rapidly from place to place.

Daytimes there were nearly always the thin rippling cries of cranes flying south, and at night he heard the wild geese honking.

The horses began now to show their long shaggy winter coats. Even the blind colt had lost his sleek summer look. His mane was grown out, his neck had lengthened, and his body more nearly fit his legs. His tail, that had been no more than a little brush covered with tight short curls, was now growing long and swishy like any horse's tail should be.

The cool days filled all the colts with excitement and they ran and snorted and kicked and bit, from the pure fun of using such lively bodies.

Often in the mornings when they came to drink they found ice around the edges of the water holes and white frost topping the grass in the low places.

By now the wolf pups were beginning to run with the old ones, learning to kill, and scarcely

a night went by that they didn't hear the howls of the big "grays."

And then one night, when it was clear and cold, with a bright full moon, the blind colt mixed with the wolves himself.

The horses had moved down into the broken country of the Badlands to get out of the wind. They were scattered around over the flat floor of a little canyon, some lying down and some asleep on their feet, when an old mare on the outskirts of the band snorted in alarm. In an instant every horse was on his feet, wide awake.

A pair of old gray wolves and three pups had been creeping towards them from the downwind side, to keep the horses from smelling them. But a sudden eddying of the wind around the wall of the canyon had brought their scent to the old mare. Now the band was alarmed, only waiting to see just where the danger was before they started to run.

The wolves gave up their creeping tactics then and made a sudden rush for a yearling standing alone on the side nearest them. There was a moment's confusion; then the horses were thunder-

38

ing down the canyon and out on the flat, a solid black mass of flying manes and tossing heads in the moonlight. The wolves had missed the yearling and now were close on the heels of the running horses.

As long as the band ran closely grouped as they were, there was nothing the wolves could do but follow until some began to straggle.

For a mile or more they ran, and then they came to a place where the ground was rough and broken by side canyons and small buttes of one kind and another, which were bound to divide and scatter the running horses.

Seeing what was coming, the brown mare whirled to the right, desperately trying to break back to the open flat. But she found the way blocked by the wolves; so she turned the other way and swung up a side canyon that seemed to lead up to the rimrock and the open country above. The other horses were already gone. The mare and colt galloped between the steep canyon walls with all five wolves at their heels.

Before they had gone more than a little way the mare found that their road to escape was a

trap instead. For it turned out to be a box canyon with high walls all around and no way out except the way they had come.

Crowding the colt into an angle of the canyon wall, the mare whirled at bay between him and the wolves.

In spite of the fact the horses were fighting for their lives, it was comparatively quiet there in the moonlit canyon. The only sounds were the snorting of the horses and the soft thud of their feet. The wolves panted quietly as they sat on their haunches looking the situation over, or padded warily around trying to find a way past the mare's sharp hoofs.

For a time the horses were safe, but it looked like only a matter of time until the repeated attacks of the wolves would tire her. Sooner or later, while she was drawn to one side by one wolf, another would find an opening to slip behind her for a slash at her haunches where the great tendons are. For that is the wolves' way. If they can cut the tendons, the horse, hamstrung, is no longer able to fight and the kill is only a matter of minutes.

The fight had been going on for perhaps a quarter of an hour, and the mare as well as a couple of the wolves showed the marks of it, when an interruption came from a most unexpected source. A small washout in one wall of the canyon had at some time been used for a wolf den, and at the entrance to it was a wolf trap, set and forgotten by some wolfer long before. It was so caked with rust that all the man scent had long ago disappeared; the wolves paid it no mind. Spring floods and summer rains had washed silt and trash into it and over it, blocking the pan until it was entirely harmless.

But the mare in her first rush up the canyon had kicked it out into the open, and the wolves had since been running back and forth over it, every time shaking loose a little more of the trash that clogged it. At last one of the pups, happening to step squarely on the rusty pan, was surprised by a loud snap and the feel of the steel jaws gripping a front leg just above the paw!

The squall the pup sent up turned the attention of the rest of the wolves away from the horses. As they gathered around the trapped pup, whin-

41

ing and whimpering, the mare made a break for the open, with the colt close behind. Bowling over a straggling pup that got in the way, they galloped down the canyon, leaving the wolves to solve their own problem.

By morning they had rejoined the rest of the band, none the worse except for a few small bites here and there.

From then on they stayed more and more on the open flats. For now the wolves were not content with a single kill; to teach the pups, one family group would sometimes make as many as three or four kills in a single night.

The Great Cold

After a month or so of weather that alternated between sunny, windy days and dull, sodden drizzles, the blind colt one afternoon noticed a new and disturbing smell in the wind.

Since morning it had blown cold out of the northwest, and stringy masses of dark-gray cloud scudded swiftly across the sky beneath the low overcast. This, of course, he could not see, but the strange new edge to the wind he could feel. And his ears told him of new sounds and of old ones that were suddenly silent. Magpies were squalling and bickering with a new excitement even in the middle of the day, when they were usually quiet. And the last of the meadow larks had left some time in the night for the long trip south. All day long the sky was noisy with the honking of flocks of wild geese hurrying out of the north.

His skin prickled, fluffing out his rough winter coat, and he felt full of an excitement he'd never known before. With the other colts he kicked and bit and ran and snorted in sudden fits. But the colts were not the only ones to notice the difference. The other horses, too, were skittish, kicking up their heels and running for no apparent reason.

Late in the afternoon a cold rain began. By that time the mustang band had already moved off the flats, down into the broken country of the Badlands, where they were protected from the wind.

During the night the air grew colder and the rain stopped. The colt was startled by feathery things that blew against his face and tickled his sensitive muzzle. At first he stamped and snorted, not knowing what manner of thing this might be. But after a time he got used to it, and went to sleep standing, like the rest of the horses, for it was much too wet to lie down. He had practiced the trick off and on all summer, learning to take his weight on three legs while he rested the other.

When morning came and the horses started

44

moving around, the colt was frightened by a weight of caked snow on his back. Thinking some varmint had taken him by surprise, he threw his head down, swapped ends, and buck-jumped until he'd dislodged it. The snow, which was wet and heavy as fall snows often are, had gathered thick on the backs of all the horses during the night, making them look like they wore heavy blankets.

The ground underfoot was strange to the colt, and all around him was the fresh sharp smell of snow that he'd felt in the edge of the north wind the day before. When he tried to walk, he had to lift his feet high to get through the sticky stuff. The grass, wherever it stuck up above the surface of the snow, was wet and soggy. As the horses plodded through, searching out grass that was not covered, the wet snow packed in their hoofs, until a ball sometimes three or four inches high stuck to the bottoms of their feet, making walking very difficult.

Still, it was not too cold. Although their rain-soaked coats were no protection from the cold wind, they did well enough as long as they

stayed in the protection of the Badlands. And after another day and night of steady snow, the sun came out dazzlingly bright on the white land.

In a few days the snow had melted and the country was brown again. But now the smell of snow was in the wind more and more often, and the time between the melting of one snow and the coming of another was shorter and shorter, until after a night when the snow had been sharp and stinging like fine gravel in the air, the sun came out but brought no sound of running water from melting snowbanks. The air was sharp, and stung the blind colt's nostrils. The snow underfoot did not clog and drag at his feet, but creaked and rustled instead.

Now the colt had many more things to learn as he went about the business of living from day to day. The snow was treacherous stuff, in many ways. It sometimes filled gulleys from bank to bank. During the summer he'd learned to sense these before he was in danger of falling into them, but now there was nothing to give him warning. Once in a really deep one, floundering around in the powdery snow, he would have no

hope of ever getting out. A couple of experiences with smaller ones taught him the danger here, and he came to feel out his way on strange ground carefully with his feet.

In the draws were the little seepage springs where the snow hid glasslike ice that could throw a careless horse and break his bones.

But the colt learned fast, and more and more his other senses grew sharper to take the place of his blind eyes. When the Great Cold came he was already a range-wise fellow, frisky and full of vinegar, while several of the other colts were gone to wolves, snakebite, or falls in washouts.

There were times when the snow fell steadily for days on end and the wild horses stayed close to the shelter of the Badlands, moving as little as possible. Other times unusually heavy snows and winds piled the drifts so high there that they had to move out onto the windswept prairie to find grass, and huddle up with their tails to the wind when they were not grazing.

Later in the winter, the snow was deep even on the flats, and had a hard frozen crust on top. To get to grass then, the horses had to paw

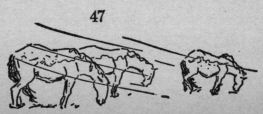

through the crust, and to break it up with their hoofs.

When the crust got too thick to be easily broken through they moved up to the tops of the rounded hills, where they had to take the full force of the wind, but where the snow was mostly blown off as fast as it fell.

Water was no problem now, although the ponds and springs were frozen deep, for the snow gave them what they needed. Grass and shelter from the wind was the big problem. And the wolves were still active, more so than in the summer. For in summer there were many kinds of small game they could get that were now holed up for the winter. And now most of the young things were nearly grown and much harder to capture. Often in the night the blind colt heard the howl of a big "gray," and stirred restlessly as he remembered his brush with them months before.

Whitey and old Spot didn't get out on the range so often now. For there was hay to haul and ice to chop at the water holes, to say nothing of the business of going to school. A needless waste of time, Whitey thought, but a fixed idea with Uncle Torwal. Now and again on a Saturday Whitey would ride out, and although he seldom saw the blind colt he often saw traces of the bunch of mustangs. Places where the snow was pawed up marked their grazing grounds. Once he saw where they had stayed in a cottonwood grove during a blizzard, gnawing the bark off the twigs because the grass was covered up.

He often spoke to Uncle Torwal about the colt.

"Too bad I didn't shoot him when I had the chance," Uncle Torwal would growl. "Prob'ly saved him a heap of misery that way."

"He lived all summer without anything happening to him, didn't he?" Whitey would always argue.

"Yeah, sure," Uncle Torwal would admit. "But you gotta remember that summer ain't winter out on the range. That little feller probably has fell in a snowdrift an' either froze to death or got wolf et by now."

"Why couldn't we bring him to the ranch and put him in with the saddle horses here in pasture?" Whitey asked. "Then nothing at all could

49

happen, and I could put in my spare time taming him."

"If I ketch that colt on the ranch eatin' good feed I'll make wolf bait of him so quick it'll make your head swim," Uncle Torwal growled. "It was bad enough that I let you talk me into lettin' him stay out in the brakes," he went on. "Anyways, I doubt that he's alive by now."

"I haven't seen him for quite a spell, but I don't think he's dead; he's too smart," Whitey said, but his lip was kind of sagging and he was feeling pretty bad.

Uncle Torwal didn't say anything more until he'd finished mixing his batch of sourdough biscuits and got them in the stove. Then, seeing how Whitey felt, he spoke up.

"I'd been kinda figgerin' you'd forgot about the colt," he said. "But if it'll make yuh feel any better, he ain't dead, or leastways he wasn't this morning. When I was out ridin' I saw him."

Whitey did feel much better then, and he quit trying to argue Confusion, the dog, out of lying under the stove where he was slowly getting his brains addled.

"How did he look, Uncle Torwal?" he hollered, accidentally stepping on Confusion's tail in his excitement.

"Purty as paint," Torwal said and added, "What in time ails that fool dog?"

Poor Confusion had been wakened from his brain-addling by having his tail stepped on, and in his hurry to get out from under he'd knocked the ashpit door open, collecting a few live coals in his hair. Not enough to hurt him, but plenty to send him jumping up on the chair where he was never supposed to go, and from there to the table where he collided with the can of condensed milk.

"Oh, his brains is just addled from sleepin' under the stove. I knew it'd happen," Whitey said. "I told you he was too smart to have anything happen to him!"

"What in the world is eatin' on you?" Torwal wanted to know. "You claim his brains is addled, and he sure is acting it, then you say you allus knowed he was too smart to have anything happen to him. It don't make sense, somehow."

"I wasn't talking about Confusion; I was talking

51

about the colt," Whitey said. "Or I was when I was talking about his being smart. Everybody knows Confusion is just a fool dog and probably has always been addled."

"Well, between you and the dog and that blind colt I'm goin' to be addled myself. I don't want to hear any more about it. If those biscuits are done let's eat — if the smell of singed dog hair don't turn your stummick, that is."

"Yessir," Whitey said, as he spread out last week's *Denver Post* for a tablecloth.

The Spring Snow

After months of cold and snow and storms, the blind colt was wakened one night by a change in the wind. At sundown the night before things had been as usual. But now instead of the bitter cold there was a warm dry wind blowing out of the northwest. It was the great Chinook wind that sometimes comes pouring from the mountains and melts the snow like magic. It whined and moaned through the windworn buttes of the Badlands, and made drumming sounds in the rimrock. It seems always to mutter strange sad things to itself as it works. Everywhere it goes it is followed by the sound of running water from melting snowbanks.

By morning there were already patches of sodden bare ground showing on the tops of the hills. Everywhere the blind colt went he heard water running. Water dripped from the overhanging snowbanks along the canyon walls, and little streams gurgled underfoot on the side hills and in the bottoms of all the gulleys.

So much snow melting soon saturated the air with moisture, making the wind seem raw and sharp. The wind blew for another day and night, and when it stopped there were great ragged patches of bare ground showing all over the country. The sun continued to shine warmly in the daytime, although the ground still froze hard at night.

Before many days the snow was gone, except for the big drifts in the deep draws and on the north sides of the hills. Faint traces of green from new grass began to show in the sheltered places. With the grass came masses of bright yellow and purple flowers. A few early meadow larks appeared, and ground squirrels woke up from their winter laziness and ran and whistled on the flats.

The beginning of spring showed in the horses' coats, for their long winter hair began to loosen and fall off to make room for the short summer coats growing up from underneath, giving them a rough and ragged look.

The blind colt often heard Whitey and Spot slogging by now, for spring brought a busy time for the ranchers. The thaw made the deep mud into death traps for stock that was weak and thin from the long winter. So they rode the range every day, trying to find and drag out bogged critturs before they got chilled through from the cold mud and died.

Just when it looked like spring had come for sure, it began to rain again. After a day and a night the rain turned to snow.

In a few hours the snow was inches deep and falling faster. At first it came in big feathery flakes, falling so thickly nothing could be seen more than a few feet off; but as it grew colder they changed to fine sharp grains that stung like shot driven on the edge of the wind. As the cold became more intense the snow became drier and finer.

The wind swirled and swooped down into every gulley and hollow, scooping up the powdery flakes from the ground and filling the air with such a choking smother that the mustangs were

unable to breathe and were driven out into the open where the air was a little clearer. Away from the protection of the canyon walls the wind was so bitter and the snow was driven with such force that the horses could not face it. There was nothing they could do but turn tail and drift with the storm.

The snow blotted out all landmarks, hiding trails and danger spots alike, but the blind colt was handicapped less than the others, used as he was to traveling where he could not see. But even so, the storm seemed to press in on all sides of him, and the roar of the wind and the rattle of the snow made his other senses almost useless, sharp as they were. He stumbled and slithered along with the rest, his back humped up and his head down.

All day the horses drifted slowly ahead of the storm, always searching for some place sheltered from the wind, and always being driven out of such places as they found by the choking, swirling snow. Out in the wind the snow blew straight ahead and breathing was a little easier.

56

Sometime during the second night of the big blizzard the mustangs were picking their way along a narrow trail leading to the rimrock, when another horse stumbled against the blind colt and shoved him off the path. He squealed and lunged, trying to keep his footing, but the steep slope offered no foothold and he slithered downwards ten or fifteen feet before he struck the bottom.

When he picked himself up he was unhurt, for the deep snow had cushioned his fall. He had fallen into the head of a gulley, and on three sides of him were walls that were too steep for him to scramble up. He floundered around in the soft snow, whinnying frantically, but the rest of the horses were already out of sight in the storm and he was left alone.

He floundered around in the snow that was belly-deep and getting deeper, trying to find a way back up to the trail. Before long he was exhausted and had to give it up. But he soon found he could not stay there. The snow eddied down into the pocket and piled up so fast that he'd soon

have been buried in it. So he started moving in the only direction possible, following the bottom of the gulley downhill.

For what seemed like a long time he struggled ahead, slipping and sliding along the floor of the gulley as it wound steeply downhill, and lunging through deep drifts and patches of buck brush hidden under the snow.

The wind whined and made strange crying noises as it curled over the edges of the banks above him. The weight of the snow in the air pressed down on him. He was soon drenched with sweat from his exertion and his terror. Luckily he was too frightened to stop; if he had, he'd have soon frozen.

The gulley he'd fallen into finally opened into another larger one. Here there was more open space and the snow was not drifted so deep, but still he could not climb the sides. All he could do was keep on drifting.

It must have been near morning, and he was weak and shaking with weariness, and his steamy breath had frozen, forming icicles in his nostrils until his breath was nearly cut off, when he sensed an obstacle barring the way. Moving cautiously up to it, he found a wire fence cutting across the canyon here. For a while he stood still against it, undecided. But soon the force of the storm drove him on and he turned in the direction that led quarteringly away from the force of the wind.

He went on cautiously, feeling a trace of a well-worn path beneath the snow beside the fence. A little farther on the fence ran uphill, but the canyon being wider here, the wind had flattened the drifts out somewhat and the blind colt was able to flounder through without much trouble. After climbing out of the canyon it wasn't long before he found that he'd drifted into a fence corner. The other fence joined the one he was following at right angles, and to go in either of the directions that were open now he had to face directly into the wind, against the full force of the storm. He couldn't do that, and it looked like he would be trapped there in the corner until he froze to death, as so many other horses would be in this storm.

But as he moved restlessly, leaning against one

59

of the fences, it suddenly fell away from him. He moved forward carefully and felt the cold touch of barbed wire around his feet. But he didn't get tangled in it and was soon safely across. The wire gate there had not been fastened securely and had fallen down as he rubbed against it.

So now he was once more in the open and could drift directly ahead of the storm. The ground here was more level and traveling much easier.

He had stumbled on for some time when a sudden lessening of the wind startled him. He stopped short and threw up his head, and shook it to free his ears and nose of snow. He knew that something nearby was breaking the force of the wind. And when he cleared his nostrils enough to sniff, he smelled horses somewhere up wind. Maybe it was the bunch he'd lost, and his mother. He whinnied and followed the smell as fast as he could, and soon came to an open-fronted shed banked up and roofed with musty hay. Inside were horses, warm and safe out of the storm.

When he came close he learned that they were strange, and he was suspicious of the unfamiliar smells of the shed. But he was tired and cold and lonely, so after a time he moved carefully into the warm darkness. But a sudden squeal and a pair of heels on his ribs drove him out.

For a time he was driven out whenever he started in among the other horses. But after a while he found himself between the wall and the side of a pot-bellied old horse that took only a half-hearted interest in driving him out, and let him alone after a few nips.

The heat from the bodies of the closely packed horses made it mighty warm and comfortable in there, and it was only a little time until the blind colt was sound asleep beside old Spot.

The Box Canyon

All the next day the storm blew, and the horses stayed under the shed, spending their time dozing or reaching their long lips between the poles that made the walls to get odd spears of the musty hay that was banked against the outside and over the roof. Now and again one or another of them would take a notion to run the blind colt out, but as soon as they quieted down he would come back to his place beside old Spot. And after a while they got used to him and didn't bother him so much.

As for Spot, he had taken a great fancy to the youngster, as an old horse will sometimes do, and the colt stuck to him like a burr.

The second morning the sun came out clear, but when the horses went outside they found the grass covered deep with snow. They wandered to the stackyard nearby and leaned against the fence, looking hungrily at the haystacks inside.

Later in the morning the blind colt heard a noise over at the far side of the pasture and threw up his head to listen. Spot heard it too, and looked up to see Whitey and Confusion, the dog, wallowing through the deep snow afoot.

The colt ran off a little way and stood snorting and fidgeting, waiting for Spot to come. However, Spot didn't seem to be alarmed, but went trotting straight toward this new danger, while the colt moved around in a circle, undecided. He wanted to get away from there, but he didn't much want to go alone, for this was a strange place and he didn't know what all was around him.

After a little, as Spot continued to trot confidently ahead, the colt followed him cautiously, stopping every few steps to snort and sniff and listen.

Whitey's excitement can be imagined when he saw it was actually the blind colt that was following Spot. He rubbed the old horse's head and talked to the colt, which had stopped some distance off. Spot looked around at the colt, as proud as if he'd foaled it himself, and Whitey

was in a swivet with excitement. But Confusion sat in the snow with his tongue hanging out and expressed no opinion at all.

Ordinarily when a stray wandered into the home pasture this way he was right away run out where he belonged. But Whitey had no intention of letting the blind colt get away, and he didn't intend to let Uncle Torwal find out he was there if he could help it. This was plainly a situation that would take some careful figuring.

He considered the matter as he threw hay over the fence and scattered it out on the snow. Now that the horses were out in the open again, they remembered that the colt was a stranger and chased him away from the hay when they could. But always the colt would come back to where Spot was, and when he learned to keep his distance from any of the other horses, he had little trouble.

After Whitey had thrown the hay out, he hung around as long as he dared, admiring the colt and trying to think of a way he could keep him without Uncle Torwal finding out about it. But after a while he had to leave, for fear Torwal would wonder what had happened to him and come out to look.

That afternoon Whitey came back again. He still didn't have a plan, but he brought a pan of oats. When he rattled them in the pan, Spot threw up his head and came trotting up. He knew what the sound meant. The colt followed at a distance, as he had in the morning. Tolling Spot along with the pan of oats, Whitey walked away from the rest of the horses. When he'd gotten Spot off by himself, he scattered some of the oats on the snow and walked off some distance and stood still.

Spot got busy right away eating the oats while the colt listened to find what Whitey was doing. Not hearing anything, he moved carefully forward a few steps at a time, snorting and bowing his neck. By the time he came up to Spot, most of the oats were gone, but he did manage to get a taste of them.

When Spot had finished, Whitey rattled the pan again, and poured out some more oats on the snow in another place, and backed off a little dis-

tance. Spot lumbered to the new pile while the colt whirled away, only to come slowly back as the boy stood still.

Whitey repeated the performance several times that afternoon, and the first thing next morning he was back again, with more oats.

Gradually the colt lost some of his fear, and after a time he would come up within a few feet and eat the spilled oats greedily. But before he got so he'd let Whitey touch him, the snow was gone and something had to be done about him if Uncle Torwal wasn't to find out.

So one afternoon Whitey brought the oats and a hackamore, caught Spot, and climbed up on his back. He rattled the oats pan now and again, and rode slowly off towards the far end of the pasture. He'd decided to shut the colt and Spot in an old corral over in a far corner of the pasture. It was hidden in a little box canyon, and with any luck it would be months before Torwal would have a reason to go near it.

The colt was somewhat puzzled by this business, but by now he had begun to lose his fear of Whitey, and the oats rattling in the pan sounded

mighty good as he followed cautiously along.

When they came to the corral, Whitey rode on into the farther side. Getting down on the ground, he stayed quiet except for rattling the oats pan now and then, while the colt came up and carefully smelled out the corral gate. He finally decided that there was nothing much to be afraid of, providing he kept his wits about him, and, standing just inside, he turned his attention to Whitey. Seeing that the colt was not minded to come any nearer as long as he was there, Whitey poured part of the oats out on the ground in a couple of piles, climbed carefully over the fence, and walked off a little distance.

At his first move the colt had whirled away, but after a little he ventured back up to the gate and snorted around until he was convinced that Spot was alone inside. After that he walked carefully up to get his share of the oats, and while he was busy with them Whitey quietly moved around and shut the gate.

Then he pushed his second-hand Stetson to the back of his head and looked through the bars of the corral at his new horse. The colt was his now, and Whitey was so full of pride that his chest hurt him considerably, and he felt like he might swell and bust any minute.

Now all he had to do was keep Uncle Torwal from finding out anything, until Whitey had the colt gentled and perhaps taught him some tricks. He figured that once he got him trained the way he wanted him, Uncle Torwal would see what a smart horse he was, and how he wouldn't be any trouble after all, and so wouldn't make Whitey turn him loose.

Whitey stayed around the corral a long time that day, talking softly to the colt, and thinking about the stir he'd cause when he went riding into town on his new horse. Now folks that had never noticed him to speak of when he'd ridden old Spot around, would point him out as being the only feller in the country who had a blind saddle horse.

He straddled the top rail of the fence and pictured himself riding up in front of the store where all the loafers were gathered, and guessed he'd teach the colt to kneel to let him get off like he'd heard the Arabs or some such fellers did. Maybe he'd give the colt his hat or gloves to hold in his mouth, while he went in the store to get Uncle Torwal's tobacco and the mail. That reminded him that he'd better ask Uncle Torwal to get him some gloves, so he'd have them when he wanted to do the trick.

From then on he spent all his spare time with the colt. Every morning he came over early to feed him and see that the water was running into the trough as it should. At first the colt ran to the far side of the corral as soon as he heard him, but always Whitey talked to him and rattled the oats pan before he poured out the grain on the ground. After a few days the colt got so he'd come up and eat with Spot, while Whitey stood quietly outside the fence.

A few days more of that, and instead of pouring the oats out on the ground after he'd rattled the pan, he poured some into his hand and stuck it through the fence. Spot right away started eating them from his palm, but the colt snorted around and was afraid at first.

But Whitey had watched Uncle Torwal enough to know that it took plenty of patience to do any-

thing with a wild horse, and after a while he had
the colt eating from his hand. From there, it was
only a question of time until the colt would let
him reach through and scratch his head or his
back.

And then one day, instead of reaching the oats
through the fence, Whitey went inside. The
change frightened the colt at first, but after a
time he came up on the far side of Spot and
reached his soft muzzle under Spot's neck for a
mouthful of oats. Whitey never moved a muscle
for fear of scaring him away, and the colt gradually became bolder until he was following the
boy around the corral like a dog.

So far everything had gone about as well as he
could ask. The colt was rapidly becoming tame,
and if Uncle Torwal had noticed that Whitey was
spending a lot of time on some mysterious business of his own, he hadn't mentioned it.

A Sunday Horse

Always, now, the blind colt was waiting for Whitey at the corral gate, anxious to smell his pockets to see what he'd brought him.

The colt was pretty well pleased with the new way of living. Whitey and Spot were both friends, and he had all he wanted to eat. He'd even gotten used to Confusion, who at first reminded him of a coyote because of the size of his noises and the smell of his fur. He knew now that the dog was harmless, and they even played games, chasing one another around the corral.

One day Whitey brought a piece of rope with him, and when the colt came up he let him smell it thoroughly, and rubbed his back and sides with it.

Before long he was able to dangle an end of it over the colt's back without his trying to buck it off. The next thing was to make a rope hackamore

71

and slip it over the colt's head and fasten it. After he was used to that, it was a simple matter to teach him to lead. Of course all this took time, but Whitey didn't begrudge a bit of it, and whenever he thought about the excitement he'd cause when he went out around the country riding his new horse and making him do tricks to amaze folks, he broke out in goosepimples all over.

Whitey's spending so much time playing with the colt and talking to him made Confusion kind of jealous, so he always got as close under their feet as he could while they were busy. And one day Whitey got an idea as he watched the colt and the dog touching noses. He carefully picked the dog up and set him on the colt's back.

The dog and the colt were both startled at first, but Whitey rubbed the colt's head and talked to him until he quieted down enough to turn his head and smell the dog. As for Confusion, he was quite pleased with himself, and sat up on the colt's broad back and grinned his long-tongued grin like a circus dog. The colt finally got so he'd let him jump up and ride around the corral on his back any time.

72

After he'd taught the colt to lead, and had him gentle enough that he would let himself be curried all over and have his feet picked up, Whitey decided it was time to teach him to come when he whistled. He turned the colt and Spot out of the corral and let them graze in the pasture awhile. Then he would rattle the oats in the pan and whistle. Hearing the oats, both horses would come trotting.

Before long they learned to come when he whistled, whether he rattled oats or not. For an hour or so every afternoon he turned them out to graze, while he watched that they didn't get out where Uncle Torwal might happen to see them.

One afternoon he was sitting on top of the old corral fence watching Spot and the colt busy grazing some distance off and thinking how lucky he was that Uncle Torwal hadn't found out what he was doing.

He was just in the middle of deciding that he'd show the colt at the county fair in the fall as a "High School" horse, and was listening to the crowds in the bandstand hollering with excitement at seeing the blind colt jump through a flaming hoop with him on his back, when he was interrupted.

"What's that little crow-bait doin' in the pasture here, Bub?"

Uncle Torwal had ridden up from the other side, and Whitey had been so busy with his county-fair imaginings that he hadn't heard him.

"Oh, he's jest grazin' with ol' Spot," Whitey said after he had pulled himself together. "Ain't he a purty scamp, though?"

Uncle Torwal got off his horse and climbed up on the fence beside Whitey before he answered. Then he took his jackknife out of his pocket and settled down to whittling like he was going to spend the afternoon horse trading.

"He is a right likely lookin' piece of horseflesh, for a fact," he said after a while. "Too durn bad he's blind, ain't it?"

"You bet he's purty!" Whitey said, and he wondered what he should say next. He knew that the time had come for a showdown, but he also knew that Uncle Torwal had his horse-trading humor on, and that there was no use coming straight out and asking him anything. So he de-

74

cided to horse trade too, and he took his jack-knife out and pried a whittling stick off one of the corral poles while he waited for Uncle Torwal to make the next move.

"Him an' Spot act like they was ol' friends. Kinda looks like the colt musta been in here quite a spell," Torwal said after a while.

"Yessir, it does kinda look that way for a fact," Whitey agreed, and whittled busily.

"Wouldn't be surprised if maybe he drifted in during the blizzard," Uncle Torwal went on.

Whitey knew that all this had nothing to do with whether he could keep the colt or not. Uncle Torwal was just playing cat and mouse with him, and he'd have a lot better chance of keeping the colt if he could keep on acting like a horse trader. So he tipped his old hat a little farther down over his eyes and whittled some more, like he wasn't worried at all.

"Yessir, that's probably just about what happened," Whitey said.

"Now that he's made up to ol' Spot the way he has, it's kinda too bad we gotta shag him back out on the range again," Uncle Torwal said.

"Yeah, it does seem kinda too bad, don't it?"

"Of course, if he was gentle an' knowed anything, it'd be different," Torwal went on. "But you take a crittur raised wild like he was, and bein' blind too, I doubt that a feller would ever be able to do anything with him."

"But you figger that if he could be gentled he might make a good Sunday horse?" Whitey asked, grinning privately to himself.

"Well, I dunno," Torwal said. "But when I was a kid I had a blind saddle mare, and she was a dandy. Sure-footed as a goat, she was. An' never ran into nuthin'.

"But she was extry smart," he added after a little thought.

"This colt is mighty smart, just like I always said!" Whitey exclaimed.

"Well, he did manage not t' get wolf et, or fall into nuthin'," Torwal agreed. "But that was prob'ly jest luck. It don't mean he could learn anything else."

Whitey saw that now was the time for him to get busy if he wanted to keep the colt. So he slid down off the fence.

"Watch this," he said, and whistled shrilly.

The colt stopped his grazing and came trotting up. When he got close he smelled Torwal and snorted and stopped. Whitey called him and the colt came on, keeping his ears pointed at Torwal, however, and snorting a little.

Whitey fed the colt a handful of oats and put the hackamore on him and rubbed his hands all over him and picked up his feet, one by one, to show that he was gentle, like he'd seen horse traders do.

Uncle Torwal sat quietly so as not to upset the colt.

Then Whitey called Confusion and patted the colt's back. Confusion came running and jumped to his place on the colt's back.

"How you like this, Uncle Torwal?" Whitey asked as he led the colt up, with Confusion still riding.

"Well, I'll be dogged!" Torwal exclaimed. "Don't know as I ever seen anything like it before."

"Oh, he's a smart feller, all right," Whitey said, grinning fit to split his face.

"Durned if he ain't," Torwal agreed. "Kin he do anything else?"

Whitey had hoped Uncle Torwal would ask that, because he had spent a lot of time teaching the colt a special trick for just such an occasion.

He turned to the colt. "Do you think you could ever learn to be a fancy saddle horse?" he asked him, and scratched him lightly between the forelegs. The colt nodded his head up and down.

"You ain't going to be any trouble to anybody, are you?" he asked him again, and at the same time he scratched the colt's shoulder. The colt shook his head sidewise.

"See that, Uncle Torwal! He can even talk!"

"Durned if he can't!" Torwal grinned. "Reckon he's smarter than I figgered."

"Yessir!" said Whitey. "An' he'll learn to do a lot of other things, too!"

Uncle Torwal climbed down off the fence and walked over to his horse.

"Well, you better bring him home and put him in the calf pasture if you figger on keepin' him," he said as he climbed into the saddle.

"Yessir! I'll bring him right over!" Whitey said.

Just in case you might think that maybe a blind colt would not be able to do all the things that this one did . . .

Back in the spring of 1917 or 1918 or thereabouts we had a blind range colt on the ranch in Montana. We found him under much the same circumstances Whitey and Torwal found this one, and much the same argument came up about shooting him, with the same result.

He ran all summer with the other range horses in the Badlands along the Powder River and didn't get "wolf et" in spite of all predictions to the contrary. And even when the bands were rounded up and ginned around through gates and corrals for the periodic government inspections that were necessary at that time, he came to no harm, avoiding fences and other obstacles with apparently no trouble at all.

The fact that he is not still alive was due to an accident that no horse could have avoided, and had nothing to do with his being blind. And he was a smart little feller.

My father claims that years back, when he was not much bigger than Whitey, he had him a blind mare for a "Sunday horse," and was the envy of the country roundabout.

GLEN ROUNDS

Rapid City, South Dakota
April 4, 1941